Originally published as *Luuk en Lotje: Het is kerst!* in Belgium and Holland by Clavis Uitgeverij,
Hasselt—Amsterdam, 2018
English translation from the Dutch by Clavis Publishing Inc., New York

Visit us on the Web at www.clavis-publishing.com.

Luke and Lottie: It's Christmas! written and illustrated by Ruth Wielockx

ISBN 978-1-60537-491-8 (hardcover edition)
ISBN 978-1-60537-501-4 (softcover edition)

This book was printed in June 2019 at Nikara, M. R. Štefánika 858/25, 963 01 Krupina, Slovakia.

First Edition
10 9 8 7 6 5 4 3 2 1

Ruth Wielockx

Luke and Lottie

It's Christmas!

Clavis
NEW YORK

It’s almost Christmas!
“Today we’re decorating the Christmas tree!” says Lottie.
“But first we have to pick out our tree,” Luke adds.

“Are you two ready to go?” asks Dad.
“Yes!” Luke and Lottie call together.

Luke heads to the biggest tree at the farm.
"I want this one," he says, pointing.
"That one is too big!" Lottie says with a laugh.
"It won't fit in our house."
Luke and Lottie find a perfect tree for their living room.

It’s beginning to snow.
“Look,” says Lottie. “The trees look so beautiful covered in snow.”
“All the trees except for our tree,” says Luke.
“It’s still green and empty.”

"Well, let's decorate it!" suggests Mom.
Luke and Lottie hang the shiny ornaments on the lower branches.
Dad helps them with the higher ones.

"The tree still looks a bit empty," says Luke.
But Mom knows what to do about that . . .

"We'll bake Christmas cookies!" says Mom.
Luke and Lottie cut out stars, hearts, and gingerbread men from the dough. They make a hole in the top of each cookie. When the cookies are ready, they will put a ribbon through the hole. Then they can hang the cookies on the tree.

"All we have to do now is turn on the lights," says Mom.
Three . . . two . . . one.
"Oh!" Luke and Lottie say together.
Hundreds of twinkly lights shine on the Christmas tree.
Mmm, and the tree smells good. Like cookies!

Time to get ready for dinner.
Luke and Lottie put on their nicest clothes.

“My bear can come too,” says Luke.
“And I’ll take my doll,” says Lottie. “Everyone will join the party!”

Ding-dong! Grandpa and Grandma are here . . . with presents!
Luke and Lottie put the presents under the Christmas tree.

Dad made a delicious Christmas dinner.
Grandma and Lottie clink their glasses together. Ting!
Luke puts his glass in the air. "Merry Christmas!" he calls.
Whoops! Watch out, Luke — don't spill.

Time to open the presents.
Everyone gathers around the Christmas tree.
"Look! Red slippers. My favorite color," says Lottie. "Thank you, Grandpa."
"Oh, new pajamas! Thank you," says Luke, and he gives Grandma a hug.

All the presents are unwrapped.
Dad and Grandpa are singing Christmas carols by the fire.

"Christmas Eve is the best night of the year," whispers Luke.
"I agree," Lottie says.

Everyone has gone to sleep, but Luke and Lottie sneak downstairs.
"I have a present for you," Lottie whispers.
"I have a present for you, too," Luke says softly.
"But . . . that's your doll!" says Luke.
"And this is your bear!" Lottie says with a laugh.
Merry Christmas!